BULLY AT SC

A Bully's Perspective

Written by:
Nia Mya Reese

ISBN:
Hardcover - 978-1-948282-24-6
Paperback - 978-1-948282-23-9

BULLY AT SCHOOL: A Bully's Perspective

Yorkshire Publishing
3207 South Norwood Avenue
Tulsa, Oklahoma 74135
www.YorkshirePublishing.com
918.394.2665

ACKNOWLEDGEMENTS

I would like to thank my Mommy, Daddy, and Faith Chapel for a **LOT** of tips on helping me to deal with people. Thank you to Deer Valley Elementary, and all of my teachers for teaching us how to deal with bullies.

Finally, I would like to thank my cousin Faith Martin, who has given me illustration ideas for both of my books.

Once there was a girl in the 4th grade named Shelia. She was a very respectful girl to adults, but there was one problem, she bullied kids at school every single day.

She didn't know why, but she did.

She would TEASE kids, FROWN at them, and sometimes she would PUSH and YELL at them when they wouldn't play with her.

She really just wanted friends but she didn't know how to make them.

One day, Shelia was walking in the hall and noticed a girl named Debbie grabbing her stuff to put in her locker. Shelia went over to speak to her but Debbie knew who she was and put her stuff in her locker and ran to class.

Shelia ran after her, just to speak, but Debbie didn't know that. This made Shelia SAD.

The school over-speaker said "PLEASE HURRY TO CLASS!"

Debbie stopped running when she saw her classroom, but Shelia was far away from her class. Shelia started running but she got stopped by a familiar face. It was Principal Christina. She told Shelia to stop running.

Shelia said "but Debbie was running too". Principal Christina said, "maybe I will talk to her later, but YOU stop running"!

Shelia felt EMBARRASSED and ANGRY so she stopped running and was very late to class. She was just trying to speak and now she was late.

Shelia's 4th grade teacher Mrs. Chrystal asked Sheila why she was late. Shelia said she did not know. Mrs. Chrystal told her to sit down and then told everyone to open their math books to page 192. Shelia opened her math book to page 192 and saw something she had never seen before.

It looked very CONFUSING.

Shelia thought, "this doesn't even make sense to me". She was also very BORED. Shelia didn't want to do the classwork, so she raised her hand to go to the restroom to get out of doing the classwork.

"Shelia didn't you just use the restroom a minute ago?" said her teacher. "Oh ok, clumsy me", said Shelia. She said "never mind". "Ok" said her teacher and she continued to teach.

Shelia then thought of another excuse — she asked for some water.

Her teacher said "ok Shelia" so she went to the water fountain and took a few sips of water from the fountain.

Once she came back it was time for lunch. When they got to the lunch table, Shelia sat alone. Nobody wanted to sit by her.

Shelia felt very SAD. So she sat down and ate her sandwich, chips, juice, and cookie that her parents packed for her.

She had a silent lunch and a SAD one.

After lunch, Sheila went back to class. Although her teacher Mrs. Chrystal was really nice and loved her, she still felt SAD.

Her teacher noticed it. Shelia really wanted some friends. As Shelia was "dreaming", the teacher called Shelia over and asked

"Is something wrong Shelia"?

"Well...no" said Shelia.

"Come on", said her teacher.

"Ok, I'm SAD" said Shelia.

"But why" asked her teacher. Shelia answered, "Well kids keep running away from me."

"Well have you been mean to them?"

Shelia answered "Yes...but..."

"Shhhhh..." said her teacher.

"Listen... treat others the way you want to be treated."

Shelia had never heard that before.

When it was time for her to go home, she sat on the bus alone on purpose.

She was thinking about what her teacher said. When she got home, her mother was ready to hear about her day.

Shelia quickly asked her mother about "treat others the way you want to be treated".

Her mother explained that it means that if you want people to be nice to you, then you must be nice to them.

"Oh", said Shelia. Shelia then put on her walking clothes and went out for a walk and thought and thought and thought about what her mom and teacher had said to her.

When she came back it was time for bed.

Once her mom kissed her goodnight and left out of her room, Shelia went to sleep. She dreamed about what her mom said.

The next morning at school, Shelia helped her teacher clean the classroom.

When she went back into the hall for water and saw Debbie, she SMILED at Debbie. Debbie SMILED back.

Debbie saw that Shelia had changed - just by SMILING at her.

So, Debbie went to talk to Shelia, and soon they were laughing and became friends.

Debbie then introduced her to more friends and Shelia was never friendless again.

THE END

TIPS FOR BULLIES TO MAKE FRIENDS:

1. Try smiling at people and not look so mean

2. Say "sorry" to whoever you have bullied

3. Try to start a conversation

4. Find out what you have in common
   with the other person

Nia Mya's BIG TIP: I know that you are sad, but try not to spread it. Instead, tell an adult.

TIPS FOR PEOPLE BEING BULLIED:

1. First, ignore them

2. Then walk away or move away

3. Then get an adult today

4. Then say "stop" in a firm way

Nia Mya's BIG TIP: First try being nice to them and if that does not work, follow the steps above.

I hope you liked this story and I hope that it helped you understand how bullies feel on the inside, how to deal with them and if you are a bully how to stop being one.

Love,
Nia Mya

CPSIA information can be obtained
at www.ICGtesting.com
Printed in the USA
LVHW070242050219
606427LV00020B/544/P

9 781948 282239